The Giant and the Big Project

Send all inquiries to: Carson-Dellosa Publishing, P.O. Box 35665, Greensboro, NC 27425.
Made in the U.S.A. ISBN 978-1-62399-164-7 01-122137784

This will be the perfect place to hang Audrey's sign, the Giant thought as he pulled up to the library. *I'll put it on the community bulletin board.*

He parked his bike and hurried in with Audrey's sign in hand. "Dog Walking by Audrey," the sign announced in large, colorful letters.

One sign on the bulletin board caught the Giant's eye. "Help Needed to Build a Community Garden," it read. "All donations are welcome."

Hmm…a community garden, the Giant thought. He pictured himself digging in the dirt, planting carrots and tomatoes. *That sounds like fun*, he decided.

The Giant couldn't wait to get started. But the garden was not built yet. The organizers still needed money.

I know how I can help right away, thought the Giant. *I can make a donation!*

"Guess what?" the Giant asked excitedly when he got home. "The town is building a community garden, and I want to make a donation."

"What's a community garden?" Audrey asked.

"It's a place where everyone can grow vegetables and flowers," the Giant answered.

"Sounds good," said Alex. "How are you going to earn the money?"

"I'm not sure," the Giant admitted. "It's a big project to do all by myself."

"Don't worry," Alex and Audrey said. "We'll use teamwork!"

That night, everyone sat at the kitchen table. Audrey made a dog-walking schedule. Alex and the Giant thought of ways to earn money.

"How about a lemonade stand?" the Giant asked.

“Good one!” Alex replied. “Let’s put that at the top of the list.”

Soon, they had a long list of ideas. Their favorites were a lemonade stand and a car wash.

The Giant got up early the next day to make lemonade. He mixed up a batch and tasted it.

Too sour, he thought. He added some sugar and tasted it again.

Mmmm, delicious, he thought, smacking his lips. *I'd better make a lot. Everyone will want some.*

Before long, there was lemonade everywhere!

The Giant set up his lemonade stand in the front yard. A next-door neighbor was his first customer.

"Thank you," she said. "This lemonade is delicious. I'll tell everyone to stop by."

But, after waiting all morning, the Giant didn't sell another cup.

"I think you need to advertise," Alex suggested, "like Audrey did for her dog-walking service."

"That's it! Teamwork!" the Giant cried. "Let's use Audrey's dogs. We'll help each other."

Alex and the Giant helped Audrey attach bright signs to the dogs' collars.

"Make sure everyone sees the signs," Alex called out to Audrey.

The Giant watched as Audrey and the dogs took off down the street. Cars honked, and people waved. *This is a great idea*, he thought.

“Oh, no!” Audrey cried when she turned the corner.

Audrey saw not one, not two, but *three* other lemonade stands, each bigger and fancier than the Giant’s. *No wonder no one is coming to the Giant’s stand*, she thought.

When the Giant woke up the next day, he saw that it was pouring rain outside.

"I guess we won't be able to have our car wash today," said Alex sadly.

"Maybe it will clear up," the Giant replied hopefully.

But it just kept raining.

“I have the perfect idea for a rainy day,” Audrey said when she saw how disappointed the Giant was. “Let’s make cookies and hold a bake sale!”

“Let’s do it!” the Giant agreed, feeling better already.

Alex and Audrey tried to remember what they had used the last time they baked cookies with their grandmother.

As they called out ingredients, the Giant poured them into a large bowl. He added flour, salt, brown sugar, eggs, and a few other things he found in the kitchen.

Then, they took turns stirring the thick dough.

Finally, the cookies were ready. Alex and the Giant each took a big bite.

"Yuck!" they said at the same time. "These taste awful."

"Oh, no!" Audrey cried. "Maybe we should have used a recipe."

"Now how will I earn money for the garden?" the Giant sighed.

"Don't worry," said Alex.
"We'll think of something else."

Audrey thought of a way to cheer up the Giant. "It stopped raining," she said. "Would you like to help me walk my dogs?"

While Alex cleaned up the kitchen, the Giant and Audrey collected all the dogs. She was up to seven dogs now, almost more than she could handle.

"Let's work as a team," the Giant suggested. "You walk the smaller dogs, and I'll walk the bigger ones."

The two walked the dogs all around the neighborhood. With the Giant's help, all the dogs walked in the same direction. Their leashes did not get tangled.

"Thank you!" Audrey told the Giant. "This is so much easier with your help."

When Alex heard about how well the walk went, he had an idea.

"Why don't you and Audrey work together?" Alex asked the Giant. "Then, Audrey will have help, and you can earn money for the community garden!"

"As a team, we could do more than just dog walking," Audrey said. "We could wash and groom dogs, too. We've had lots of practice with Oliver."

The two made a new sign and a plan to divide the work and the money they earned.

The new business was a big success!

Audrey signed up new customers while the Giant walked dogs. Audrey washed dogs, and the Giant brushed them.

Before long, both partners were earning money.

A few weeks later, Alex helped the Giant count his money. The Giant couldn't believe how much he had earned.

"Excellent!" the Giant sang out as he did his favorite happy dance. He couldn't wait to donate the money for the community garden.

The Giant felt very proud as he gave a fat envelope full of money to the head gardener.

"My goodness, this is a heavy one," she said. "Be sure to write your name on it. A plaque in the garden will show the names of everyone who helped make it possible."

The day the community garden opened was sunny and warm. Alex and the Giant joined many others in planting neat rows of vegetables.

"It's beautiful," Audrey remarked when she stopped by with Oliver.

Alex and the Giant wiped dirt from their hands. They stood up and admired all the good work they had done.

"Come on," Alex said to the Giant. "I want to see your name on the plaque."

"There it is!" Audrey exclaimed, pointing to the Giant's name. "And our names are right next to yours!"

"Surprise!" the Giant said. "Teamwork made my big project a BIG success. I couldn't have done it without you!"